This book belongs to

....

This edition published by Parragon Books Ltd in 2017

Parragon Books Ltd
Chartist House
15–17 Trim Street
Bath BA1 1HA, UK
www.parragon.com

Illustrated by: Gavin Scott
Reading consultant: Geraldine Taylor

ISBN 978-1-4748-9520-0

Printed in China

My First Storytime
Jack and the Beanstalk

PaRRagon

Bath • New York • Cologne • Melbourne • Delhi
Hong Kong • Shenzhen • Singapore

Five steps for enjoyable reading

Traditional stories and fairy tales are a great way to begin reading practice. The stories and characters are familiar and lively. Follow the steps below to help your child become a confident and independent reader:

One day, Jack's mum said, "We have no money and nothing to eat. Take our cow to market and sell it so that we can buy some food."

Jack took the cow to market. He swapped the cow for some magic beans.

8

Step 1
Read the story aloud to your child. Run your finger under the words as you read.

Step 2
Look at the pictures and talk about what is happening.

Step 3

Read the simple text on the right-hand page together. When reading, some words come up again and again, such as **the, to, and**. Your child will quickly get to recognize these high-frequency words by sight.

Jack ran all the way home with his bag of beans.

9

Step 4

When your child is ready, encourage them to read the simple lines on their own.

Step 5

Help your child to complete the puzzles at the back of the book.

One day, Jack's mum said,
"We have no money and nothing to
eat. Take our cow to market and sell
it so that we can buy some food."
Jack took the cow to market.
He swapped the cow for some
magic beans.

Jack ran all the way home
with his bag of beans.

But when Jack's mum saw the beans, she was cross.

"Silly boy!" shouted Jack's mum. "Now we have no cow, no money and nothing to eat!"

She threw the beans into the garden and sent Jack to bed.

Jack went off to bed. He was sad about the beans.

The next morning, Jack looked
out of his window. There was a giant
beanstalk in the garden! Jack was
hungry. He climbed the beanstalk
to look for some beans to eat.

He climbed up and up,
into the clouds.

Jack went all the
way to the top of the
giant beanstalk.

At the top of the beanstalk, Jack found a giant castle. He knocked at the castle door. The cook opened the door.

"Please can I have something to eat?" said Jack.

The cook gave him some food. Then they heard footsteps.

"You must hide!" she cried. "The giant who lives here likes to eat little boys for his supper!"

Boom, boom, boom! Jack hid in
a cupboard.

The bad, greedy giant stomped
into the kitchen.

"Fee-fi-fo-fum, I smell the blood of
a little boy!" the giant shouted.

"Don't be silly," said the cook,
"you can smell sausages."

Jack was scared. Would the giant
eat him?

The greedy giant ate his sausages.

"Bring me my gold!" roared the giant. The cook got his gold and the greedy giant counted it.

Soon, the giant fell asleep. Jack popped out of the cupboard and grabbed a bag of gold!

Jack quickly climbed back down the beanstalk with the bag of gold.

Jack's mum bought some food. But soon, all the gold was gone and they were hungry again. Jack climbed up the beanstalk again.

He hid in the castle. Soon, the greedy giant came into the kitchen.

"Fee-fi-fo-fum, I smell the blood of a little boy!" he shouted.

"Don't be silly," said the cook, "you can smell meat."

The giant ate his food.

"Bring me my hen!" roared the greedy giant. The cook fetched a fat, red hen. The hen laid a big, golden egg!

As soon as the giant fell asleep, Jack popped out and grabbed the hen.

Jack climbed down the beanstalk
with the fat, red hen.

The next day, Jack climbed the
beanstalk again. He hid in the castle
and waited for the giant to come.

"Bring me my harp!" roared the giant.
The cook got a golden harp. The harp
sang to the giant. He fell asleep. Jack
popped out and grabbed it. But the
giant woke up.

"Fee-fi-fo-fum!" he cried.
"Stop! Come back, boy!"

Jack climbed down the beanstalk
as fast as he could go. The giant
chased after him.

Jack got to the bottom and grabbed
an axe. He chopped down the beanstalk.
Crash! The giant fell to the ground.

And that was the end of the bad,
greedy giant.

Puzzle time!

Which two words rhyme?

top   can   fum   mum   bed

Which word does not match the picture?

bean

magic

cow

Which word matches the picture?

gold

hold

told

Who hides in the castle?

Jack

giant

mum

Which sentence is right?

The giant said fee-fi-fo-fum!

The giant said fo-fum-fee-fi!